KAZBEK

KAZBEK

A NOVEL

LEONARDO VALENCIA

TRANSLATED FROM THE SPANISH BY HILLARY GULLEY

Autumn Hill Books

This is an Autumn Hill Books book
Published by Autumn Hill Books, Inc.
1138 E. Benson Court
Bloomington, IN 47401 USA

First published in 2006 by Funambulista as *Kazbek*
© 2006 by Leonardo Valencia

ISBN: 978-0-9987400-7-2
Library of Congress Control Number: 2019949615

Cover design – Justin Angeles

Interior design and layout – Rose Wehrenberg
rosewehrenberg.earth

KAZBEK

We must be on the lookout, said Luder. Day or night we must never stop searching for a window through which to make our bold escape into the unknown.

Julio Ramón Ribeyro, *Dichos de Luder*

I

Mr. Peer gave Kazbek a camel leather portfolio containing sixteen drawings of insects. Mr. Peer wanted to make a Small Format Book, in which each drawing would be accompanied by a text. Kazbek could write whatever he wanted. He could even turn the text into something more than a commentary on the drawings.

Kazbek examined each drawing and began to wonder what, exactly, was a Small Format Book. The next day he returned to Barcelona, placed the portfolio on a shelf and forgot all about the drawings Mr. Peer had given him in Guayaquil.

✿

The insects had been drawn in black ink on white paper in December of nineteen ninety-nine. Mr. Peer had used a Mitsubishi Uniball II micro. He had been inspired by the inhabitants of Quito and their fear of the Pichincha volcano eruptions. Mr. Peer referred to the insects as *vermin*. He said they lived in the darkness of the volcano and crawled out because of the eruptions, though he didn't know if it was before or after the eruptions, or before and after the eruptions. He began to draw them with the idea that he would send them out as Christmas cards to a limited circle of friends. But as he drew he realized they were becoming something he should not give away, though he couldn't say why. Mr. Peer exorcized his fear of the eruptions, completed the drawings, tucked them into a manila folder and thought, No one ever knows who they're working for.

✿

Was Kazbek the intended recipient of that failed Christmas giveaway? Or were the drawings only passing through his hands as part of their metamorphosis? What is it exactly that Kazbek will deliver to Mr. Peer once he has written the texts, if he ever does?

What Kazbek really needed to do was finish the novel he had been brooding over for the past several years.

✿

Mr. Peer believes that as an artist, he must be held to nothing more than coherence with himself. That is why readers should receive an artist's work as a gift that will only sabotage their hunger. When the reader wants something concrete, when the artist considers the reader's wishes and creates with these in mind, art has perished, according to Mr. Peer. He thinks respecting the reader would be like handing him a mirror so he can see his own face at the cost of concealing the horizon.

✿

Nine months later, despite repeated attempts to write during the day and at night—especially at night—Kazbek remains unconvinced by the pages of his Great Novel. His main character, Dacal, is eluding him. He realizes his project has failed. While arranging his papers he finds the portfolio with the drawings by Mr. Peer. He opens it, studies them and thinks about how he doesn't like the word *vermin*. He sees the insects as beetles. Then he wonders what use his words could possibly be to these drawings. And then he takes the thought even further: what use could the rest of his words possibly be at all? He had hit bottom. If he kept thinking this way it would be the end of him. Still, Kazbek is skeptical of the expression *to hit bottom* because it is a metaphor. He knows that in language this bottom is nothing more than silence and that silence, sooner or later, will be broken, even if not by words. He decides the best thing to do is to go outside and get some air at the café by the sea. On his way out the door the phone rings. The kind of call, he thinks, that always seems most urgent and imperative. It was probably Isa who, yet again, could not resist calling him from Guayaquil outside of their pre-scheduled times.

✣

Mr. Peer was born in Berlin. He received his training in art schools in Dresden and Paris. In nineteen sixty-two he went to live in Ecuador, the country traversed by volcanoes, which was how he described it to his German friends, evoking the words of Humboldt. This was the same country where Humboldt had studied the light, the flora, and the fauna. Mr. Peer appropriated aspects of local culture. He did so freely, precisely because this was not his land of birth and he was not a local artist. In reality, he was fleeing monsters who, though they seemed dead, were still hiding in Europe. His eyes yearned to rest, so he filled them with his new country's light and animals. He made drawings of flora and fauna that were full of color, with round, pleasant shapes, reds elevated to pure ardor and yellows the essence of a sunflower field. And the flora and fauna were forever transformed by him. Many followers of his work traveled to the country traversed by volcanoes because of Mr. Peer's drawings. But after a few days they would grow disillusioned. The fauna—iguanas, crayfish, pangules—and the flora—mangroves, cacti, ceiba trees—didn't have the same pure colors and soft contours as the ones in the drawings. The followers had chosen the wrong journey: they had traveled to the land itself and not to the imagination of Mr. Peer.

✿

Mr. Peer wants his vermin to keep scurrying around in the darkness so they can later surface on the page. Who knows where or in what form they'll surface? Like always, as the reader concentrates on the steps of one character, the others don't cease to advance. To imagine a correspondence in the general progression of the characters is the challenge that time presents to readers' minds. Time turns readers into travelers in search of light. Time surreptitiously carries readers to a simultaneous vantage point at the apex of their memories. Characters in the book are also travelers in search of light, but it's different. They are bearers: on their shoulders they carry the readers' worlds. The vermin will advance, they'll surface on the readers' skin and arrive at the center of the readers' brains, which boil with luminous connections and, sometimes, dark light.

✿

The caller was not Isa, but the character who had been tormenting him for years and about whom he had failed to write his novel: Dacal. Kazbek doesn't know how to say no to him and accepts his invitation to meet at the café by the sea. This is no fantasy, nor is it a case of a rejected character, like the ones in Unamuno or Pirandello. Dacal is his old boss from his advertising days. Kazbek and his friends—also disciples of Dacal—wrote a series of stories about him. They never signed their names to them. They wanted to remain anonymous because they were choral stories, narrated in plural, to which each contributed their own point of view. The group dispersed around the world and Dacal went to Lima. Only one member of the group had been in touch with him again, because Dacal had also moved to Lima. Through this friend, who had asked to remain anonymous, Kazbek discovered that Dacal had gotten his hands on their stories about him. Kazbek asked how Dacal had taken them. The anonymous friend said he didn't know. Dacal had taken off for an area south of Lima to live near Nazca, in the Ica desert.

✧

In Paris, in nineteen sixty, Mr. Peer acted in a play written by Picasso: *Le Désir attrapé par la queue.* In gratitude, Picasso had given him a signed copy of a book of etchings: *Suite Vollard.* Picasso's handwritten dedication had omitted a letter of the artist's real name, baptizing him as *Monsieur* Peer. Once the dedication had been written, the newly baptized Mr. Peer told Picasso that he had omitted a letter, and Picasso responded that it was better that way, with those two repeated letters which, like in his own name, Picasso, seemed to vibrate, lending movement to the word and opening a fissure within it. It was through this fissure that the most radical experiences of dreams and imagination could enter (or escape). Mr. Peer accepted the name given to him by Picasso. They never saw each other again.

❂

What is a Small Format Book? Kazbek asks Mr. Peer. He responds point by point with a total of nine approximations. He says that it is:

1. A short book that never seems to end.

2. A book that can never be lost because it will never be forgotten.

3. A book that, like a knife, slices into the closed body of the Library.

4. A book that doesn't have any pretension of delivering a Great Final Blow.

5. A book that awakens the reader's curiosity about its author, who until then has remained completely unknown.

6. A book that the reader never expected to find.

7. A book that no one knows how to categorize, nor what the critics have said about it, nor who published it.

8. A book that the reader cannot summarize without subverting and destroying its content.

9. A book that creates a silence so the reader can hear how the fountain flows.

❖

Dacal continues to elude Kazbek. Why is he able to escape? Kazbek thinks the image that guides him—a man lost in a desert—is purposely avoiding narration. Dacal in the desert is an instant of pure dissolution, where there is no milestone, no climax that *explains* his decision to retreat to a tiny village in the Ica desert. As if he were resisting the novel's causal connections, the character has chosen an elusory place so he will be left in peace. He can't be narrated in the desert, Kazbek thinks. And even more interesting: *he doesn't want to be narrated.* He only wants to speak his own words. He, Dacal, is the narrator, the one who constructs his own sequence of words. Perhaps the gregarious spirit within his group of friends, which took the form of a plural narrator, could capture Dacal in the brief plot of a short story. All they did was quote the things he said. Still, Kazbek suspects there may be another formula. He thinks: only a man can follow another man and return with the message. He repeats this again and again like an incantation he doesn't understand: *only a man can follow another man and return with the message.*

The phone rings. Kazbek checks his watch. Now, yes, this should be Isa.

✤

There are four themes in Picasso's *Suite Vollard* etchings: the sculptor's studio, reinterpretations of Rembrandt, rape, and the Minotaur. But there are two dominant themes: the sculptor's studio (forty-six plates) and the Minotaur (fifteen plates). The theme of the Minotaur is different from the lewd versions of the satyrs, with a human

head, horns, and legs that taper into hooves. The Minotaur, on the other hand, has the savage figure of a bull for
its head and, in some cases, a human face. The Minotaur
is not savage: its bullhead is a violent crown on a perfect
body. But the Minotaur cannot free itself of its own head.
Picasso creates beauty he does not understand, he creates
monsters and labrynths to defend what he does not understand. The etchings of the *Suite Vollard* are trials, approximations, the free movement of biting acid on a plate
displacing his concerns about the creative process. *Suite
Vollard* is a book with limited circulation. The sequenc-
ing of its themes follows the movement of the spirit that
inspires it, without aim or purpose. They are the traces of
metamorphosis. They are *animantias*, living things. The
artist always captures them, like desire, by the tail. And at
the last possible moment.

❖

Kazbek tells Mr. Peer that the nine points defining a
Small Format Book are true. He also asks whether he had

intentionally offered nine points instead of ten. Perhaps he did it that way to be asymmetrical. Mr. Peer replies that symmetry is essential and that, in contemporary art, a work must be composed so that it appears to be asymmetrical. He mentions artists like Palazuelo, Chillida, Gaudí, or Greenaway. Or musicians like Mompou. And, adds Mr. Peer: always hide the part that completes the symmetry so that it can be revealed at the right time.

Still, Kazbek insists on knowing what the tenth point is.

I'll tell you, says Mr. Peer. But promise me you'll never put it in writing.

Kazbek promises.

Mr. Peer tells him.

❂

When Kazbek received the drawings, another volcano had begun to erupt, the Tungurahua. The writer had spent days in the vicinity of the volcano. He had walked in its rain of ash blown by the wind and felt the ash in his throat and then he lost his voice. He would stop speaking for the next several months.

What had happened to produce this correspondence of two volcanoes erupting that caused Mr. Peer to draw and Kazbek to receive the drawings and set out to write? Kazbek thinks this has to do with Mr. Peer, who trembles along with the volcanoes and has now opened a door for him to enter this trembling. In his way, he has saved him from the desert he was becoming by writing about Dacal. He thinks. And he thinks that artists need to establish milestones like the boundary markers of an imaginary ring. Once in place, a movement commences that makes the markers spin at a great speed, until they form a ring. And it is in this ring that the fight begins.

II

Ambroise Vollard was an exemplary editor. There were two reasons for this: his risky bets and his discretion. The son of a notary, he moved to Paris to study law. But during his strolls along the banks of the Seine, while stopping to flip through the books and paintings of the *bouquinistes*, he discovered his passion for art and books. He took a job in a gallery. During his constant browsing at the *bouquinistes*, he found a book in octavo with a stamp: *Ambroise Firmin-Didot éditeur*. Vollard immediately understood his destiny. His name was also Ambroise, and he wouldn't be hurting anyone by becoming an editor. In fact, he did a lot of good, because he would begin to work with the painters he knew and ended up publishing the most important painters and illustrators of the early twentieth century. He published Verlaine, illustrated by Bonnard, Alfred Jarry, also illustrated by Bonnard, Balzac, illustrated not by Bonnard, but by Picasso—who should have been the one to illustrate Jarry, but Vollard was not perfect—and he commissioned Braque to illustrate the Theogony and Chagall to illustrate Gogol's *Dead Souls*. Vollard was never able to brag about being an editor of bestsellers because he never made bestsellers, but he took risks for some of the most innovative artists of his time and for the least conventional books. His only desire was to be remembered as an art dealer. Perhaps that's why he managed to become one of the most indispensable editors of the twentieth century—because he wanted to be remembered for something else. His only autobiographic work is entitled *Memories of an Art Dealer.*

❀

Unlike Mr. Peer, Kazbek was born in the country of the volcanoes. He left in nineteen ninety-three and only returns on occasion. His characters are almost always errant types. He feels as if he has not invented a thing: he has only lent words to what he has seen and heard during his time. He would prefer not to be so uprooted and to have a house of his own. The books he has written he built as if they were houses where he could take refuge from the devastation of the world's motion. He has lived for many years with his manuscripts and publishes them when he senses that his residence in them is only temporary. When he received the portfolio with the drawings, the writer was about to construct his next house, something he was calling his Great Novel. But before he began, in order to rest and catch his breath, he took a trip to Lisbon.

☼

In Lisbon, Kazbek neither rests nor recovers his breath. In fact he almost looses it: he suffers a bout of delirium at the end of Rua Garret, on his way down to the Baixa Chiado metro station. Through the silence and the dark night and the lost looks of the noctambulant Lisboans, the depth of the big escalator leading down to the station seems like the mouth of hell: it's interminable and ominous.

Something happens after this shock. Many questions come to him. Does what he write really turn into a house? Does he write because of an acquired impulse or is it a siren song that leads him to a false home? Without a home, without his Great Novel, the writer clings to the words that in this moment he remembers having heard from a great poet: when the volcano roars there is still time for dance, song and poetry. If the lava comes, said the poet, it will take us at our best.

✿

There is a plaza full of insects. Concretely, beetles. At the center of the plaza, the beetles crawl up the body of a seated man with no face. The man says: *What resided in your beginnings is asking to return*. But the man can't go on. The beetles have filled his mouth, he falls to one side and they devour him. The next day the plaza is empty and no one remembers the incident. What was it that the man had said?

*

There had been a first book, unsigned, that Kazbek constructed early in his career and that is no longer in his possession. In fact, he never owned a copy. Kazbek was twenty years old when, at the advertising agency where he worked, they put him in charge of a book that would include photocopies of artists' paintings and his own texts. He had only fifteen days. To write it, Kazbek left Guayaquil for a house in the mountains—a first connection between his writing and his uprootedness—where he wrote texts, rewrote others, and transcribed quotes in order to complete the book by the agreed deadline. The manuscript became a luxury edition, the kind they give as gifts for the anniversary of a press. His memory of the words in the book is bleary. What's more, the writer was not credited on the cover. Kazbek only remembers the title: *Man and Im-*

age. He is afraid to encounter this book again, he confesses to Isa, like someone who is afraid to meet a lost brother. She thinks: *I'm going to find that book.*

✦

It's not water that baptizes but the word that names. Mr. Peer is in need of new words, just as he had received one from his teacher, who changed his name. The artist, the kind that works with images and colors—that is, in the absence of words and sounds—is precisely in need of words. To give drawings to a writer, thinks Mr. Peer, is a request for baptizing. It's also a baptism for the writer: the object gives rise to an all but unknown world.

One must then free the word that gives a breath of life to the vermin seeking their path. The word that not only speaks of movement but that is movement: the word in metamorphosis: a living thing.

✦

Kazbek travels to Tunisia for work. Once he has fulfilled his obligations he takes the weekend to relax in Sidi Bou Said. He leaves his hotel on rue de Palestine and walks in the direction of Habib Bourguiba. He contemplates the billboards in Arabic and French. They are faded and coated in dust and smog. At the intersection with Ibn el Jazzar, there is a crumbling house with peeling shutters. Against a wall there are the cracked leather chairs of the shoeshiners. Kazbek feels as if he is in Ecuador. Is it because next week he'll be travelling to the country of the volcanoes? When he reaches the station, he buys a ticket and boards a train that is about to leave. He crosses the Lake of Tunis and passes through little villages along the route to La Marsa: La Goulette, Le Kram, Salambó, Cartago, Amílcar and, finally, Sidi Bou Said. In Sidi Bou Said there is not more dirt: the streets are clean, the planters full of flowers, the walls white and the doors and windows are hues of silver. The changes in the light take Kazbek by surprise. That night he sleeps soundly, in the air fragrant with traces of the jasmin that the roaming vendors sell to tourists during the day.

✿

The path toward the light, thinks Mr. Peer, does not consist only in pure contemplation of the light. Contemplation will also illuminate what it collected in the darkness of the path. That's why the path toward the light ends in the oblique: it illuminates the past and the unforeseen. But is there any light that leads to another path that leads to another light that leads to... so that everything can remain illuminated? Could this light be a voice? A few words?

✿

When he rises, Kazbek takes a taxi to visit the ruins of Carthage. He observes little of his surroundings because he has been restless from the instant he woke up. On the esplanade on Byrsa Hill the wind draws him out of his daze and reminds him that he has come to visit the ruins of Carthage. The wind is not cold but Kazbek still shivers as he opens his eyes. There is no one around. It's not high season. He looks at the ground: dry weeds, remnants of rock, half-restored mosaics. He looks into the distance: parched fields rustling in the wind. Beyond he can make out the poorest neighborhoods of Tunisia and there, to one side, the houses and mansions of business owners, diplomats, and bureaucrats that surround the presidential palace of Ben Alí. Underneath all those structures, his Tunisian friends had told him, there were still ruins of Carthage that had never been excavated.

⚜

Kazbek looks back down at the ground. His neck feels heavy. He's cold. A beetle crawls along the edge of a crumbling capital and freezes at the height of a nearby stem. The beetle has crowned its piece of column and looks in Kazbek's direction. It raises its tiny legs as if it wants to feel the speed of the wind, and this makes Kazbek imagine that the beetle is delivering a lecture. But then a gust of wind attacks, and the beetle immediately lowers its tiny legs, clinging to the surface of the stone to avoid being blown away. With this gust, Kazbek feels a melancholy that he has never experienced before. Why has he come to such sad ruins? It would be best to leave immediately and go eat some nice gilthead at La Goulette. When he gets up, the wind begins to blow hard again. He has to brace his legs. Out of curiosity he looks at the beetle. Shaken by the gust, the vermin opens its wings, lifts its tiny legs, and flies away, away with the wind.

That night, Kazbek dreams that a man is devoured by beetles.

✿

The day after the beetle nightmare, Kazbek is convinced he will write Dacal's story. For the first time, he'll abandon the chorus of friends with whom he had written the other stories. And what's more, he won't write a short story. It will be a Great Novel. He realizes the best way to tell his story is through the experience of this friend of his who wishes to remain anonymous. Kazbek will see Dacal through the eyes of this friend, his arrival in Lima, his discovery of the desert. Yes, Kazbek is convinced that he must narrate Dacal's story in a relatable register: through the eyes of an anonymous friend, whom he will call the Traitor. Because it seems that he cannot look at Dacal straight on. Perhaps because he also did not look at people straight on and went in a thousand circles with his stories. The novel will be, then, the story of a double betrayal. That of the friend in Peru who broke the pact of writing about Dacal's adventures in chorus, and the even bigger betrayal, that of Dacal himself, who betrayed his country. This time Dacal would not escape: Kazbek would catch him by the tail.

✿

Mr. Peer was uncomfortable with Giacometti's response to the criticism that his paintings, with a single central figure, were always gray. "If I see everything in gray," said Giacometti, "including all the colors I've experienced that I want to reproduce, then why should I use another color?"

Mr. Peer always used many colors, but now that he's creating a more personal work, he has been invaded by the color black. This need to reduce materials in order to ex-

pand expression is also in some of Picasso's work and in
the last lines of Moró and Fontana on white canvases. The
colors, the flourishes, had been a necessary celebration in
the past. But not now. Mr. Peer is happy with black and
white. He lives a secret celebration and repeats to himself, like a litany, what Baudelaire said: *real illustrators are
happy with their pencil.* Words are also written in black.
That's why he wants to give his vermin some words. But
he doesn't want to be the one to write them. He believes he
has already written them by drawing.

✣

When Kazbek thinks about his Great Novel, he walks
along the shelves in the library like someone doing calis-
thenics and caresses the spines of the books. Kazbek has
read several novels that were useful to him and that he
should probably reread: *Don Quixote, Lost Illusions, Doc-
tor Faustus, Tristram Shandy, Lord Jim, The Alexandria
Quartet, Moby Dick, The Sea of Sirtes, Conversation with
the Catedral, Of Heroes and Tombs, Palinuro of México,*

Horcynus Orca, Ada or Ardor, The Satanic Verses, The Unconsoled. They were all thick novels. He touches them with veneration. If there was a temple of fiction these would be its columns. But he stops walking when he finds a slender exception, standing stubborn like those little houses in the midst of skyscrapers: *Pedro Páramo.* Kazbek says it's an exception to the tomes and his own opinion. For years he has thought about organizing his library and getting rid of books that he would never read or that did not interest him—especially all those little books, booklets and anything else that could not even stand in the shadow of a column at the temple of fiction but that instead would occupy its bottom shelves—but he never got around to it.

❊

Now he wants to focus on his Great Novel about Dacal. He thinks that in order to succeed, it won't be enough to correspond with a few friends. He has to feel the air and the dust and the light of the place where he met Dacal. He would travel to the country of the volcanoes and dedicate one month in Guayaquil to finding out more about him. It would be best if he could find someone who could recount a few first-hand stories, an old colleague from Dacal's advertising days: Mr. Peer.

III

The artist's journey has three stages, thinks Kazbek, who is thinking about Mr. Peer. During the first stage, artists devour everything around them with their eyes and ears. When everything at hand has been exhausted as a source of inspiration—family, friends, place—the adolescent artist goes elsewhere to seek more nourishment. In the next stage, that of adaptation, artists search for harmony with the world because they know they can't take it all on. So they adorn it and make it shine with a definitive intensity that seduces many followers. The third stage consists in proving that they have in turn become a source of nourishment for the world and that they are a specimen on their way to extinction. That's when they emit the cry of the cannibal's prisoner, the earth trembles and their followers disperse. As of that moment their work can only interest a different type of follower, and never those who have accompanied them up until that point. But they are no longer thinking about followers. They count the days they have left as their visions advance.

❖

During his month of research, Kazbek meets with Mr. Peer three times.

The first meeting takes place on a terrace at the Tennis Club. Upon entering the club, Kazbek sees Isa again for the first time as Mr. Peer is coming toward him down the stairs. How long had it been since he'd seen her? Two, three, five years? In Isa's smile there are two rows of dancing girls dressed in white that suddenly stop. What are you doing here, you hack? Isa asks him. Kazbek barely manages to respond that he is meeting Mr. Peer before the same, like a big friendly bird, lands a hand on each of their shoulders.

Maestro, says Isa, since when are you cavorting with local hacks? Isa is terrible, says Mr. Peer, but so charming. Kazbek promises to call her. After Isa leaves, they continue to talk about her. *She's like a volcano*, says Mr. Peer. Kazbek nods and then they get down to business.

Mr. Peer has brought a copy of Kazbek's latest book so he can sign it. Kazbek, touched, gives Mr. Peer a camel leather portfolio he bought in Tunisia.

❊

The second meeting takes place at Mr. Peer's office. That's where Kazbek receives, in return, the same camel leather portfolio, this time with sixteen drawings inside.

❊

During the two meetings, Kazbek only obtains one fanciful fact about Dacal. The fact wasn't even from Mr. Peer. It was just a rumor he had heard. Dacal had worked for the Secret Service. For what country? Kazbek asked. No one could say for sure. Maybe Chile, maybe Ecuador, maybe Peru, maybe the CIA. It was probably all just a question of bad blood, slander, says Mr. Peer. The fact that he had up and left the country made room for all sorts of assumptions. This idea of incompleteness, of being surrounded by voids, awakens Kazbek's imagination. It's a hotbed of pulsating possibilities.

❖

Kazbek thinks Mr. Peer's observation that Isa is like a volcano is true but incomplete. She's more like a volcano that was dormant and that now, just like that, has become a concern or is on the verge of awakening. It's been such a long time now that Isa has been across the ocean, far away from him, and when he goes back he only meets with her to ensure he hasn't lingered too long on a volcano with signs of eruption. Kazbek is learning to be much more attentive, day and night, to the signs that will launch him into the unknown.

✿

Ever since he left his country, Kazbek made the occasional trip back to Guayaquil to visit his parents. Such that his return always becomes a celebration he tries to avoid. He's surprised to see that his parents have stuffed a folder full of his clippings and reviews and articles and interviews and placed it in his room. Many of them are now yellowed, and he doesn't recognize himself. He has resigned himself to becoming a character defined by the assumptions that half the world likes to make on the basis of the slightest indication or none at all. He observes each clipping, and he asks it to tell him what he said or thought, what he loved and hated or said he loved and hated. So he prefers not to look at the clippings and spends most of his time outside of his room. He goes out to the garden behind his house and swims in the pool, reads or contemplates the mangroves in the estuary. It has been years since he has lived with these luxuries. Hanging off the edge of the pool, he discovers an iguana sitting on a branch of a willow tree in the garden. Nearby, there's a little honeycomb, and some bees buzzing around the little hexagonal cells. But it's the iguana that draws his attention. It's as though it is petrified and, most of all, it is looking straight at Kazbek.

✿

The iguana's gaze makes him uncomfortable. He gets out of the pool and shoos it away. But it doesn't move. So Kazbek picks up a rake and hits the trunk of the tree. He avoids the honeycomb. The iguana remains immutable. Kazbek gives up. He gets back in the pool, hangs off the side and steadily contemplates the iguana. He imagines the iguana is speaking to him, asking him what he is doing there, saying he doesn't belong there anymore, that his parents are no longer his parents, and that he has abandoned them. Kazbek does not try to defend himself and allows the iguana, in his fantasy, to proceed with its accusations. The iguana seems to be saying that Kazbek will get nothing out of having returned to look for clues for his next Great Novel because *what resided in your beginnings is asking to return.*

Kazbek already knows this somehow. But where has he heard it before? It slowly comes to him that it was in the dream he'd had in Tunisia after visiting the ruins of Carthage. He looks back at the iguana. But it has darted away from an uprising of bees and is now scuttling off, shaking its tail. Kazbek feels a chill through his body and gets out of the pool.

His only plans are an outing with Isa and a third meeting with Mr. Peer. After that, he'll go back to his routine in Barcelona.

❖

Without knowing they would, the artist and the writer hit it off. Mr. Peer is much older than Kazbek. The difference isn't that apparent, since Mr. Peer has a young spirit and Kazbek, when he speaks, does so in a meditative tone that suspends any conjectures about his age. And so, during their third meeting, they begin to speak about art. That is, art created by those who no longer live in their native countries. Maybe that's why they get along so well:

they share a secret uneasiness. They know they've ex-changed their places of origin and work. They conclude nothing but do become friends. Mr. Peer criticizes Europe and Kazbek criticizes the country of the volcanoes.

Kazbek says, I've never heard people repeat the name of their country so often. Here it even shows up in the soup.

Mr. Peer interrupts him to ask whether he had just in-voked the name of his country in his own criticism. Kaz-bek maintains that he did not.

Of course you did, says Mr. Peer. You erased it from your map and filled the map with your own words. Like those portolan charts that mark the outline of the coast with names for each point. But your country will return like a *pentimento* in a painting. It will be a stain, a phantom figure.

That's more like it, says Kazbek. A phantom country.

✺

No so much a country, says Mr. Peer. And hardly a phantom. This is what I wanted to talk to you about. Dacal is a step ahead of you. He's the one pursuing you. He's moved to Barcelona.

✼

These are sixteen drawings of volcanic insects, Kazbek observes as he glances through Mr. Peer's portfolio. Then he recalls the names of all the volcanoes he memorized in school, back when he'd learned that Alexander von Humboldt had baptized his country as the Avenue of the Volcanoes. He recites sixteen names aloud: Tungurahua, Putzalagua, Casitagua, Cotacachi, Pasochoa, Sincholagua, Quilindaña, Antisana, Sagatoa, Atacazo, Chimborazo, Carihuairazo, Cotopaxi, Cayambe, Illiniza and Sangay. It's too far from this world, thinks Kazbek, as if it had been lost and all that remains are the nontransferable sounds of its names. So he decides not to include them in his Small Format Book.

❀

On the plane back to Barcelona, Kazbek feels another chill run through his body. He always gets chills when he's about to have an insight. He wants to dispel any bad ideas and so he repeats: *only a man can follow another man and return with the message.* And then he asks: What is this message? His only certainty is that if he sets out to write about Dacal, a fountain will begin to flow that will turn into a river that will turn into a flood that, almost unknowingly, will sweep away any discoveries in its path. Writing is not explaining, thinks Kazbek. So in his notebook, he begins to draft, in broad strokes, the structure of his Great Novel about Dacal. He draws horizontal lines to divide what will be the chapters of his book. But the plane jerks and the line he's drawing across the page curves. Kazbek, who still has chills, feels the impulse to continue these curved lines until he forms a circle. But there's so much turbulence that he stops taking notes entirely. When he gets to Barcelona he'll be able to concentrate better, he'll have a steadier hand and he won't be so cold anymore.

❧

To help with our project, Mr. Peer writes in a letter to Kazbek, you should keep in mind this triple encounter: reader, writer and illustrator. The illustrator's gaze goes from one page to the other, like from one abyss to the other, observing how the hand tears at the white page with the nib of the pen. The writer's gaze goes from one image to another, like from one character to another, and strings words between them in order to give motion to the whole. Lastly, the reader's gaze comes and goes between the image and the word, as a way of comparing them, and discovers excesses and shortcomings and sets in motion something that neither the illustrator nor the writer could have imagined. Peter Greenaway was right: *ink is the second blood of the world.* I suspect, adds Mr. Peer, that only through this triple encounter can the game keep producing networks of sense. Provisional ones, of course, but networks nonetheless. And nothing is more provisional than the drawings of my vermin, those little colorless monsters, what with my being known for my colors, sighs Mr. Peer. Yet here I am, reverting to black and white.

IV

The day of their reunion, during the first ten seconds of looking at him, Kazbek wanted to believe that the man before him was not Dacal. Why did he need to reappear and comment on how much time had passed? Was this Dacal's role? Kazbek wondered as he confirmed that yes, that man accompanied by a woman was Dacal. Was she the one with the slender feet he had written about and the reason he had stolen away to a hacienda in the Ica desert? The man who had wandered was now arriving at his meeting and still hadn't noticed that they were observing him. Kazbek reassured himself that the man only resembled Dacal. But as he approached and saw the man speaking to a woman in a kind of continuous murmur that seemed to have her hypnotized, he recognized the gestures: the inclined head, the hands that molded the absent matter of his conversation in the air, the smile in his verbal digressions. The way in which the woman noticed that Kazbek was watching them, and alerted Dacal. He was the first to open his arms and speak.

✿

Kazbek does not remember the words, but he does remember the effusive, histrionic tone with which Dacal exaggerates the slightest incident. He introduced the woman with such little enthusiasm that when he said her name, Kazbek immediately understood that she was not who he had assumed she was. Dacal had been running the women around in circles again. Circles that would be filled with what Kazbek would tell him, now that his old fabled mentor was at his disposal. The reunion happened too quickly: Kazbek's imagination devoured Dacal's every gesture as it attempted to match them with his memory of him. They exchanged phone numbers and planned to meet the following week.

❀

Mr. Peer did not believe in coordinates in life. He believed it was unthinkable that a man would sacrifice his existence with a decision that would divert him from his natural course. Now he no longer believes in a natural course. He knows that he changed his destiny by abandoning his language and his continent. What becomes of the kind of person who alters his coordinates in life? Mr. Peer could not find the answer. At least not until he drew his vermin. In the end, the coastline on those portolan charts was beyond the names that marked it. It was only a matter of time. These people end up leaving signs everywhere. Through them, one can come to know the places they've left behind. This dark world of Europe's imagination had given way to all the colors of the country with the volcanoes and emerged in these insects. After thinking of it like this, Mr. Peer felt calm. From that day on, he continued to make extreme paintings, to the surprise of his followers. They said he had gone dark again, but he felt younger and fresher than ever. He didn't feel a single obligation toward anyone.

❖

Kazbek understood everything more clearly during his next meeting with Dacal. First, this woman was not the one with the slender feet about whom, years ago, they had written their last group story. Second, Dacal had spent the last few years in the Ica desert with the woman with the slender feet. Third, he would never know anything else about that woman because Dacal wouldn't comment. Fourth, no one else from the group had been in touch with Dacal. Not even the one who wished to remain anonymous—although he lived in Lima, four-hundred kilometers from the Ica desert—was interested in seeing Dacal after visiting him a few times. It was as if Dacal had completely disappeared from their lives. Fifth, the latter is not entirely certain or, in any case, cannot be proved. Sixth, Dacal had a very distinct opinon about the stories they had written about him. Everything in them was a lie. And for this reason he thought they were exquisite. Seventh, at the end of the meeting, Kazbek knows that Dacal's proximity is going to be a problem.

❖

Kazbek takes notes about Dacal as he helps him get settled in Barcelona. He takes him to the best restaurants in the city, shows him the best coves on the Costa Brava—Sa Conca, Cala del Pi, Cala Pedrosa—and the little villages in the interior of Catalonia. Sometimes, when he goes to pick him up for a day out, he's with a different woman. But there's not even an allusion to the woman with the slender feet, much less a name or a reference. Which member of the group had found out about this woman's existence? Several years have passed. He can't remember. Between the blanks and conjecture that came and went as they wrote about Dacal, someone made a bold assumption and fiction set out on its irreversible course. Kazbek thinks that at some point Dacal will lower his guard and belie the assumption, or the story will be reinforced and all there is to know about the woman with the slender feet will be revealed. This point never arrives, and Kazbek begins to feel cold again. He tries to concentrate on writing his Great Novel. Except his concentration is broken by persistent chills, and he is barely able to trace lines across a blank page. Dacal is no longer within his own imagination, but to one side of it, strolling around the same city. Reality and fiction are together now, two sides of the same coin.

❧

On his way to the café by the sea, Kazbek walks along Passeig de Gracia. To distract himself from the people he looks to the ground, thinking of nothing in particular. He hears conversations and noises. Except that all of a sudden the voices stop and the sun illuminates the tiles along the walkway. He stops, his chin tucked to his chest, and realizes that the tiles are hexagonal. He positions himself inside one:

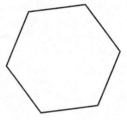

He stands still inside the six sides of the hexagon. People ignore him at first. They walk quickly past. Kazbek laughs. He has stopped, but the flow of people makes him feel as if he were creating a current break in a torrential river. He stays firm, very firm, and feels the solid pavement beneath him. After standing like this for a moment, he realizes that the perfect arrangement of the tiles has another point in common. A kind of quilted circle that spirals like a seasnail. But it is not in the middle of the hexagon. Each tile covers 120 degrees of the circle, and together with other tiles they complete the circle.

When he discovers this, his eyes pick out different circles and he is forced to move in order to connect one hexagon with another.

As he discovers other seasnails, the pavement begins
to look as if it is moving, undulating like a platform in the
middle of the sea. Or as if each hexagon were a cell containing one of Mr. Peer's insects and were about to emerge,
surfacing with their little legs and forewings in the middle
of Barcelona.

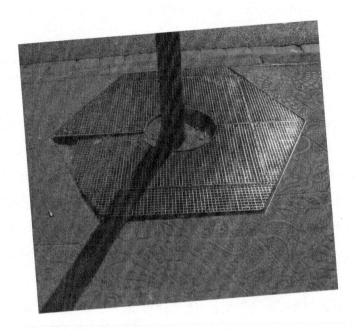

Kazbek picks up his pace, arrives at the end of Passeig de Gracia, and veers right.

Once he's on the Ramblas, he walks toward the place where he usually goes to write when he's bored with writing at home. It's a wing of an old hospital from the eighteenth century, built of stone, which was converted into a library in the mid-twentieth century. They call it the Stone Library. The wing where he always writes is called the Levante Room. It's not such a bad thing that writing surges forth in a place that was intended for healing, that it's supported by something as solid as a building of stone. Here, his characters rise with conviction and set forth. Dacal was the only one who resisted. It was as if the stone of this workspace extended to his writing hand, to the role and the figure of his character: everything was petrified. It has been weeks since he has visited the Stone Library. Now that he has given up on writing about Dacal, it wouldn't be a bad idea to go inside and say goodbye, to feel the lightness of Mr. Peer's sixteen drawings compared to the stone cold sculpture that was now Dacal, heavy as the stacks of Great Novels in his own library.

❖

In the Stone Library, Kazbek finds a copy of *Suite Vollard*. It is number one hundred and seventy-three of a total of five hundred copies printed in nineteen fifty-six. Of the etchings belonging to the sculptor's study, he's attracted to the following: the ones that include the sculptor in front of his work—usually a bust or a human body—the ones that include the sculptor accompanied by a woman and, especially, the ones that include the Minotaur. They all appear naked. The bristly head of the sculptor seems, in some of them, like the Minotaur's. The most relevant ones for Kazbek were created between the twentieth and twenty-sixth of March in nineteen thirty-three. He chooses six.

❖

He makes a note of the number and date and describes what he sees in the first four etchings, so he can think about them later at his leisure:

Number 38. Around March. Sculptor with model seated next to sculpted head on pedestal. Sculptor scrutinizes head he is sculpting.

Number 44. March 21st(?). Sculptor with basin and model squatting in front of sculpted head. Sculptor lifts basin as if offering something to sculpture.

Number 45. March 23rd. Sculptor, seated model, sculpted head. Sculptor and model look, afraid, at blank-eyed sculpture.

Number 46. March 25ᵗʰ. Young sculptor in front of bust. Title of etching says young sculptor is working on piece, but looks more like he's about to slit its throat with knife. Sculptor's eyes: sadness, nostalgia, hatred for sculpture. Crown of laurels covering sculptor's head extends to sculpture's head, like they share it. One end of crown touches tip of knife.

※

The fifth etching, unlike the rest, relaxes him. After lingering over it for some time, he makes a note:

Number 48. March 26ᵗʰ. Sculptor seated before two sculpted heads. One head—with pained expression, looks like sculptor—is pedestal for other completely different, non-realistic head, with tight skin and smiling expression. Sculptor serene contemplating two works, old and new, which is youthful and feminine.

※

The last etching intrigues him most. Kazbek jots down a brief description:

Number 86. Paris, March 18th. Sitting girl contemplating sleeping Minotaur behind curtain. Profound wisdom in girl's eyes with tenderness and fascination for enigma of Minotaur.

❁

He contemplated the etchings with a feeling of lightness. He had not been aware of how they were made. At least not until he remembers, and only then does what he has seen gain consistency: the drawings are not so light. They've been traced with a stylet on a metal plate covered with a fine layer of ground. Then the plate was submerged in a solution of water and nitric acid. The lines that remain are the trace of the drawing that is then printed. The lightness becomes substantial, thinks Kazbek.

❁

He closes *Suite Vollard*. He feels as if he has read a novel in fragments and been left to fill in the gaps. The etchings intersect in his mind and history recomposes them, again and again. Sometimes they're dense, sometimes they're light, and they always tell a different story.

✿

After returning the copy of *Suite Vollard*, Kazbek begins to feel unsettled. It's the nearby presence of those shelves filled with books at the Stone Library. Fortunately, most of the books are stored below ground. Still, he feels their presence multiplying. He collects Mr. Peer's drawings and wastes no time in leaving. It's nighttime. Dacal is surely mad at him for missing their meeting at the café by the sea. He doesn't care. Now all he wants is to go home. Then he remembers that his house is also overflowing with books. Kazbek always fantasized about throwing out all the Small Format Books in his library. He would grab a notebook and list the books he would rescue. This time it was no fantasy. And something has changed in the way he feels about Small Format Books. All books seem too heavy to him now. He marches assuredly towards the hecatomb of all the dispensable books filling his house. On the way he proclaims the titles of the books he will rescue: all will be Small Format Books. Plus, if Isa decides to come visit sometime, it wouldn't hurt for his house to be a little tidier.

❖

Kazbek places by the window tall columns of books that he has brought from the living room, the bedrooms and the study, and even from the kitchen. He looks at them for a few seconds and then begins to throw them out the window. When he pauses, it's barely for five seconds. One after the other, the books fly into the garden. Hours later, the Small Format Books he has rescued are: *Juan de Mairena, The Art of Worldly Wisdom, Silverio Lanza, Dialogues with Leuco, Luder's Sayings, Cronopios and Famas, The Secret Apprentice, Pedro Páramo, The Book of Travels or Presences, Tonio Kröger, The Stories of Mr. Keuner, Structure, The Falls, Voices, The Metamorphosis, Ward No. Six, Heart of Darkness, The Aspern Papers, The Encantadas, Ecce Homo, The Music Lesson, Sentimental Journey, A Breath of Life, Count Julián, No One Turned on the Lights, Fool's Life, Clearings in the Forest, Estuary, Jakob von Gunten, The Book of Hospitality, The File on H., Yes, The Invention of Morel, Hanged Life, The Cardboard House, The Afternoon of Mr. Andesmas, The Maker, The Monkey Grammarian, The Feldafing Notebook, Bartleby & Co., Shiki Nagaoka, The Impossible Life, Prison of Trees, Siren Twilight, Palomar, Perpetual Motion, The Cinnamon Shops, Paludes, An Evening with Mr. Teste, Farabeuf, Meditations, Praise from the Tyrant, The Plague Sower, The Secret Life of Walter Mitty, Education of the Stoic, The New Life, Journey to Parnassus, Formal Break, Varamo,* and *The Book of Monelle.*

The new library not only fits in a single suitcase but on a single page.

✿

The next day, Kazbek returns to the Stone Library and spreads out the sixteen drawings on the table. Then he contemplates Mr. Peer's vermin one by one. He contemplates them and hears a crunch. And another crunch. And another. Each of Mr. Peer's sixteen vermin has begun its exodus. There's no going back.

Without overthinking it, Kazbek begins to write.

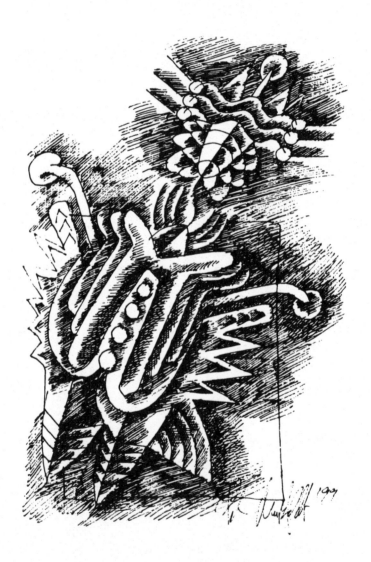

7

You crunch against the pristine page. Armed with knives, you slash our fear of the sterile. What do you seek? Not light as we see light. You seek the surface. But you who have come from the depths, you will be interpreted as a child of darkness, not as a tracer of shadows on the white page.

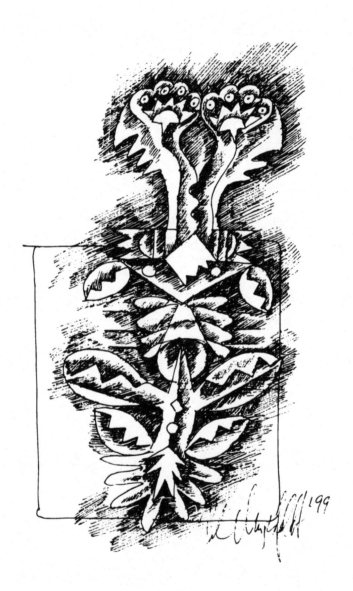

2

Your body, metallic. Your head, heavy. Your two antennas look like two four-eyed heads. But you're blind. Eight blind eyes, an excess of waste. Your body escapes its predators by blending with the inedible and deformed. Your pincers are aberrations ready to sever chains and roots. How can they break chains without being monstruous? It seems as if you might cut off your own neck to lighten your load. But you don't have to. Those who see you devour their own nightmare of references. They don't see you.

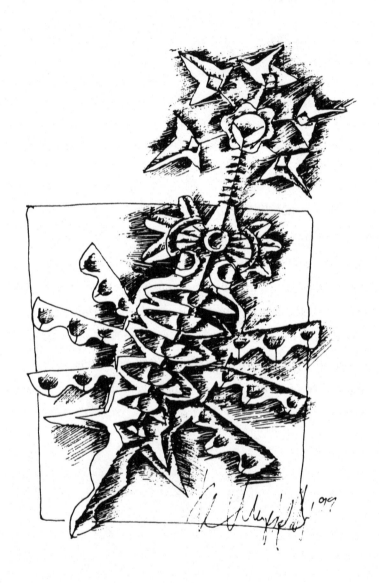

3

Each part of your body travels in a different direction. But the center's purity lies within you. Still, you overflow with doubt. Why do they expect certainty from you when your only reliable feature is your swaying face? You must fulfill an uncertain destiny and convert each step into a triumph over the unmoving. You'll be a triumph over the two-headed monster that smiles at the world with one face and bites its own abyss with the other. In that place where you rise up or fall, your crusty earthen countenance will remain, open to all directions.

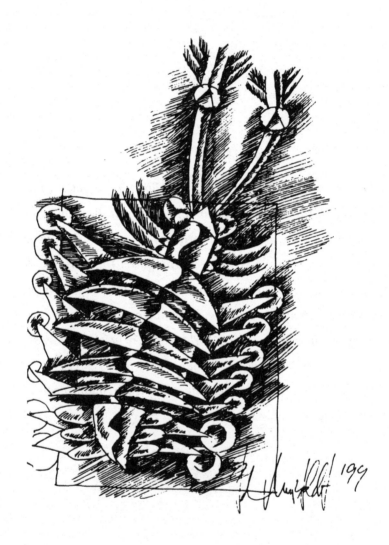

4

They can hear you. Your body crunches. The sharp spines on your back dance in a zig zag with your fourteen oval feet. Something like an accordion in your wings hums an unknown melody. Invisible to the blind eyes of your equals, your music at once calls your species to mate and alerts predators. Your song's posterity is also its death. The paradox of stridulation: you're a blind musician advancing across the mute page. To open the book is to break the seal of a sleeping volcano. Little verbless hero, you're a messenger of life and a lurer of death, the slightest sound throughout the world.

Kazbek rests. The first drafts accumulate on the desk like leaves fallen from the lush banyan tree that resembles the disheveled hair on his head. He sets aside the first four clean fragments, makes tight wads out of the other drafts, and tosses them, one by one, into the black trash can in the corner of the Stone Library. He feels light and satisfied. He craves a change of air. He leaves the Stone Library and walks to the café by the sea.

✿

Kazbek orders a coffee and stares out at the horizon. It's not the same horizon as the one in the desert where he wanted to reinvent Dacal, but its equally perfect vantage point grants him the same distance in perspective. His happiness for the first fragments makes him feel as if the world has been contoured in radiant writing.

✿

Though he knows the horizon's line is an optical effect, Kazbek feels as if he could walk toward it. He smiles like a boy at the image. A huge cruise ship crossing the Mediterranean puts an end to his good mood.

✿

The solidness of the cruise ship, unerring on its course, returns him to a critical state of mind, and his smile collapses. Maybe those four fragments are nothing. *You live in your dreams*, he tells himself. Still, he has the urge to keep writing. In addition to his surroundings, he begins to see flashes, one after the other, of new fragments.

✿

It would be best if he went back to his place, cleaned up his drafts, and sent them to Isa while he got on with the rest. He leaves a few coins on the table of the café and heads home.

5

You've lost an eye. No one notices. The circles and rectangles and triangles in your eyes hypnotize and obscure the concretion of detail. It's not even an eye you've lost. It's the geometric flourish of an antenna. Or is it a mistake left by the artist to enhance the artifice, a pentimento as part of the whole? We've seen so much, yet nothing at all, if we don't return to what we have seen over and over to mine the impression and subsequent apparition. You've lost an eye, which is like saying there is no more symmetry. With just one eye, with just one leg, with just one hand or with the shadows you trace, it is enough to scratch at the world's legible surface.

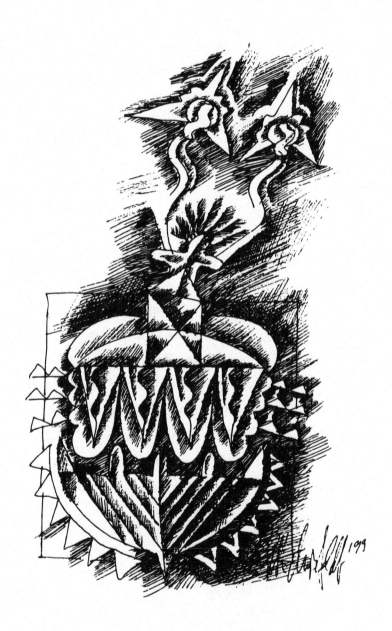

6

Magical is the moment when your extremities unfold and the world stirs to life. You move from your assigned place in search of one of your own. Why do you fear moving? Perhaps because you cease to be the domestic bait that affords survival to the rest? Or is your fear of moving that terrible moment when you discover your prostration in the clichéd? The farther from your beginnings the longer the string and the harder it becomes to tense it. Your body fits within the quadrilateral drawn in ink as your origin. Your head does not: your antennae reach forth, teasing you out of stillness, and your prickly extremities, newly emerged, cut an imaginary space that also does not belong to you. Be light, go forth on your journey. Far away from here, you will live on.

7

Black is a celebration on white and the forms that are born dream colors in the shade. Feet like palms, antennae curved by gradations in pigment, sinuosities in search of gradations of light. We will see nothing of you until you arrive at the surface. Color hardly matters: your hues do not disguise your fleshless form. To capture the writing you were drawn in black. What dark sun has traced you? What fire transports you to the unknown? Ask no more. On the surface your predators will assign you easy colors of prey. Now, live your secret celebration. On the white you trace lines upon lines, later, open to the unexpected, these lines will make for other worlds. The marks of your movement are the skeleton of a black rainbow. You will never be a wieldy sort of form.

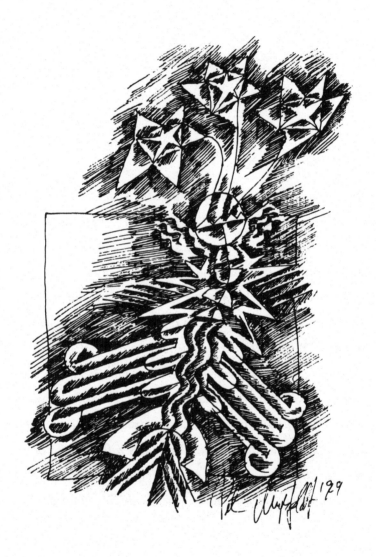

8

Your spine is crooked. What supports you? The impulse of not knowing your own nature. A perpetual movement in search of a feeling you don't know if you'll attain. You're incomplete. That's why you're a wonder to be avoided: a strange creature that marks your own beginnings. You travel from the world you abandon to the world you conquer. You live each second on the outskirts of fiction. At the cost of destroying your form, the cord in your crooked spine will be the ink for another writing. Still, you don't offer the crunchy trace of the three colorless flowers you wield above.

Isa still hasn't commented on Kazbek's first four fragments. To remind her, he sends her the next four. He immediately regrets it. Maybe he shouldn't have sent them, he
thinks. Between him and Isa there is a pull that the fragments could either accelerate or radically disrupt. For the
first time he's made the mistake of sharing writing that is
still open for changes, incomplete. She could take refuge in
the argument that it is still in progress to avoid offering her
definitive opinion. Again the huge white cruise ship, with
its unerrant trajectory, appears in Kazbek's mind, making
him doubt his ability to improvise as he goes along. What
he should really do is call Dacal to apologize for standing
him up at the café and then read him the first four fragments directly. A little display of fiction performed for a
fictional character who has escaped him.

✿

He calls Dacal and lets it ring. He calls back and then
decides to forget it. After five minutes his phone rings. *That
must be Dacal*, he thinks. But it isn't. It's Isa. She wastes

no time in telling him exactly as he feared, that though she liked what she read—even if the fragments seemed abstract without the accompanying drawings—she doesn't understand why he addressed the vermin directly, why the use of the second person? Was he sure it was the right narrative mode? He tries to explain, but she cuts him off and insists that he save his explanations for later, for now he should think about mode. She thinks Kazbek is really writing about himself. In any case, she thinks they sound like ramblings. The cruise ship, says Kazbek, it's so solid, and I'm so far from that. What? asks Isa. Nothing, it's nothing, Kazbek mumbles. Let me know when you've thought about it, says Isa. For now I'll read you something I came across after I read your fragments. Who wrote it? asks Kazbek. Just listen first. Isa clears her throat, and Kazbek can hear pages turning.

❖

I found it, says Isa. Listen:

No one knows who drew these. / We don't know why

these drawings adorn / the blurred suburbs of the void. / We don't even know if our eyes are the right ones with which to see them.

Kazbek is moved. He asks her to read it again, accentuating each pause. Isa reads it again and, as he hears it, the cruise ship in Kazbek's mind fades as if it were a ghost ship. But then he wants to know who wrote the words. I'm not going to tell you now, says Isa. Just take them in. You can't do that to me, he insists. Of course I can, she responds. I'll tell you in person, next week. What do you mean, *in person*? Kazbek asks. I'm going to Geneva to see my sister and nieces. I suppose you'll come see me now that I'm crossing the Atlantic. Kazbek says he will. I'll be at Route de Valavran 85, says Isa, and she adds: I'll tell you the author's name just before you leave.

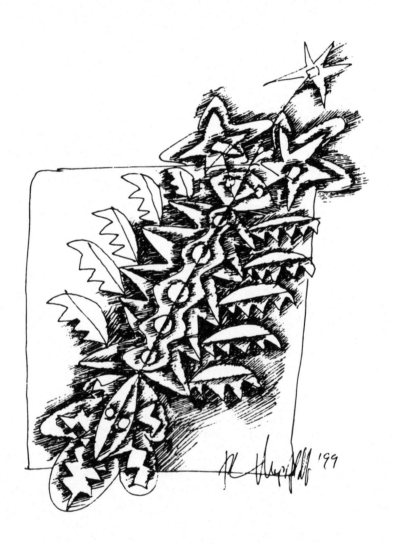

9

You spill off the page. Have we forgotten your life's three-way junction? The artist's hand and the gaze of the reader and these words that attempt to approximate your slippery form? Are you forced to insist on your condition as a fictional character? The artifice of language undoes itself to reveal more artifice. What lies outside the frame is also fiction. The hands of the artist and writer never form their lines horizontally. The page must slant to the left, one of its corners aimed at the heart of the artifice, and the hand will extend the traces of ink. In this way you trace your own fantasy of black light. When you're done, the page returns to the horizontal. It seems everything is made up of pretending, subsurfaces, the coordinates of art that sustain you. Your body is a florid spear that gouges the flesh of appearances.

10

Creature of the air. Kite of a Chinese boy dreaming of drag-
ons tamed by a string. Your antennae are like windmill
blades. Palms that resist the terror of a storm on the coast.
What are you? Into what have you transformed? How to
name you? Taxonomy's skittish beauty cannot detain your
perpetual shifts. You're an ungraspable animal for anyone
who baptizes you with a dead language. Paradox of art: live
traces invoke what has vanished and transforms it into the
unexpected. Your singular condition does not permit the
convention of a name. That's why we insist against the wind:
verbal defeat is the guarantee of life. Better to let the sparks
of analogy fly: palm, windmill, kite, dragon.

77

You advance, your body swollen with memory, and forget that there can be no adventures with too much luggage: your provisions impede your discovery of new ones. Exploration is the sister of hunger. You also insist on crowning yourself with a simulacrum of flowers. Or are they stars traced from the two five-pointed seals you flaunt atop your crowned pyramidal body? This bulge with lettuce and cauliflower folds warns of your conversion into vegetable when you reach the surface. You should never come up if it means having roots and a definitive form. Rootlessness is the brief life's path of fire.

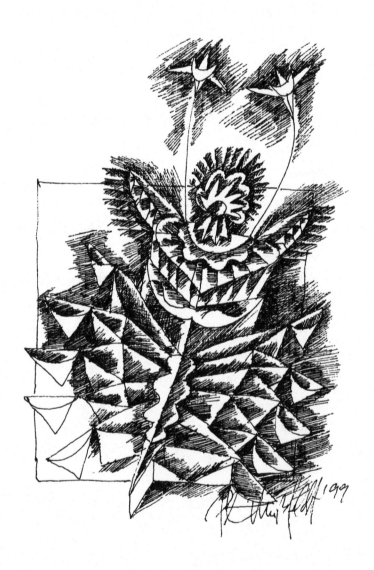

12

Your antennae bloom above you. Your legs move with the rhythm of a spider running scared. You're an adolescent animal: you want to reach the summit to see the landscape hidden by a mountain. But you don't see the top. The white page is not just blind. It's the summit and the abyss. The page's whiteness dissipates in shadow and the writing transforms into night.

Still no sign of life from Dacal. Why this affinity for elusion? Kazbek has the sudden suspicion that he is the one with the affinity for elusion, that with Mr. Peer's drawings he has raised a wall inside his own library, that if not for Isa's calls he would have completely lost touch with the outside world. He urges himself to be done with these fragments that no one is waiting for except Isa and Mr. Peer. Kazbek's urgency is nothing more than the impulse of death that always looms over him, threatening the completion of the Small Format Book. Kazbek is a larva that must choose between urging itself out of its cocoon and lying in reach of its predators. And now he scares himself: he's thinking about himself as if he were one of the vermin. Could Isa be right about his choice to write in second person? Is he really writing about himself? It's too late to change it now. Or perhaps not. Kazbek knows that it's never too late and that writing is always a draft of itself or a future book. The defining rule of his game: to be on the lookout for an ever-absent word. What he needs now is another opinion. But this time he'll only show someone after he has finished the four remaining texts.

13

You'll soon surface. Your body takes its shape. The flowers you carry with you will be an offering to the air and the light. Now you wait for the colors of life and prepare to abandon the chirping of your parts. How difficult to leave your old form. Your menacing pincers have folded into halfmoon leaves. You have forms that suggest a balance you don't yet understand. How many drafts, how many changes of skin along the way were necessary to arrive at something that has always been in you, something you blindly brought this far? In your place of origin you ran a greater risk: a closed space. You suspected your roots were thirsting to be planted.

14

Of course, you're the big joke. You move your little legs to seek attention and isolate the readers from the world's stage. Why do you need to transpose real-life events onto the page if the page of the world is already overflowing? Your fate is another, at the margin: you strip the word of its routine and drown the tension of the possible. A peculiar form that breaches the moods of melancholy. Black on white: sketch and writing to say that it wasn't so hard after all, that your alert little legs are like the hands of a child that have been soiled from molding, without purpose or intent, a game of shadows.

15

Don't rush. Never rush. To throw so many flowers at the same time is to run the risk of blooming inconsistently. Who told you the world ends here? You still haven't thought about the possibility that the flowering garden you are becoming is a dream. Your steps are light, a handwritten draft, a writing that is drawn in search of a feeling as it appears on the paper and transforms. Don't rush. You're on the path.

16

Don't look back. All that is born is born for the unknown. Don't ask if this was the place, if this was the form. Let the world run through you until you find the place where you fit. Crowned with your imperfect flowers, you still don't know whether your feet are wings or leaves, if you're a monster, a shrub, or a scribble. Affirm yourself as writing does: add contrast to the page's blinding glow. Black light.

VI

Dacal told Kazbek he was staying on Socorro Street. When Kazbek finds himself in front of what should have been a stately home at the address in question, all he finds is a shop selling jewelry and handmade crafts. In the fall there aren't many people in Tossa de Mar, and this is one of the few businesses still open. He asks for Dacal and they tell him to go up to the second floor. He hasn't changed a bit, thinks Kazbek. Still resistant to a good clean hotel. Kazbek knocks on the door and is greeted by a teen-aged boy whom he barely recognizes. It's Dacal's oldest son, tall and lanky like his father, but with Germanic traces from Dacal's first wife.

The apartment has a big living room with paintings of the seaside. The biggest one is of a woman looking out to sea. But what attracts his attention most, because it is so different from the rest, is a tapestry from Paracas with the image of a man who seems to be falling into a void. Now he can't stop looking at it. The room gives way to a balcony with red tiles and a view of the sea, and from there, under an umbrella, Dacal drops the newspaper he had been reading and rises to greet him. He introduces him to his children, who appear one by one as their father calls them. Dacal hasn't lost his knack for creating a welcoming home, as if he were prepared to entertain any random stranger coming in off the street. Why then, asks Kazbek, had it been so impossible to write a Great Novel inspired by this man? What was the reason for his failure?

✣

It's hard to say, says Mr. Peer over the phone, days later. And in any case, it's useless to torment yourself over why the book you wanted to write never came to be and why another appeared in its place. Maybe the other was an illusion, the mirage of a path that gave you a broader perspective of the topography so you could orient yourself. You have to falter, go through drafts, live in the incomplete and the partial. And personally, I'm happy your other book failed, otherwise you wouldn't have written a thing about my vermin. I hope it wasn't too difficult.

On the contrary, says Kazbek. He'd never had so much fun.

Even better, says Mr. Peer, because readers notice that kind of thing.

Kazbek says he's not sure if he thought about readers at all. He even thinks he might have written it as an attack on readers.

Don't think about it any more, says Mr. Peer. Give me a few days to read them and I'll tell you what I think of the manuscript. I might even get to it tonight before bed.

❖

In perfect synchrony, Dacal and his children prepare lunch and set the table while Kazbek stands before the tapestry from Paracas with the man who seems to be falling into the void. The tapestry has vibrant shades that go from red to black to blue and combine to make geometric shapes. The man that seems to be falling has five fingers on one hand and only four on the other, which is supporting a diminutive head. Kazbek touches the rough strands held captive within a labyrinth of lines.

What looks like a man falling into the void, Dacal explains, is actually a monkey.

Kazbek does not ask how he snuck the tapestry out of Peru. As if he has sensed Kazbek's unease, Dacal changes the subject and announces that after lunch they'll go out on the sailboat. Will you join us? Kazbek offers his apologies and says he has to get to Geneva.

✧

One night, Kazbek tosses in bed, reaches for the phone and hears or dreams he hears the voice of Mr. Peer saying *what have you done, boy, what have you done.* Kazbek rubs his eyes. Mr. Peer is saying he's sorry for waking him. He was so excited to call he forgot about the time difference. He had read the texts three times and then revised a few here and there. He likes them, they're like verbal drawings, and he can even tell that Kazbek originally handwrote them. I did handwrite them, says Kazbek. They're hand-written drawings. And he adds in a fragile voice: do you think people will understand what I've written?

✿

Well, says Dacal as he closes the folder Kazbek gave him. He opens it again, gives Mr. Peer's vermin another look, rereads one of the texts and immediately snaps the folder shut as if he fears its contents might escape.

Something about your writing intrigues me, says Da-cal. You talk about light and it's as if you've drawn a black curtain. A very black curtain. It's as if you've complete-ly forgotten what I taught you at the agency about clarity. When I saw the little stories you wrote about me I thought it was strange how you described my comings and goings as snake-like, but at least a snake is visible. Even Mr. Peer has set aside his experience with clarity for this little nightmare. Where are you trying to go with this?

Kazbek barely offers a response. He looks out at the cove. Behind the red stones of the Mar Menuda Islet he watches a cruise ship appear in the distance. For an instant, the little boats moored close to shore, empty, appear to shrink in silence as a ghost passes by. Kazbek feels cold. He says that he has no idea where he's trying to go with this because he was never trying to go anywhere to begin with.

✿

Who cares if people don't understand, Mr. Peer responds. What we should concern ourselves with is the fact that this exists, as it is, supported by our own plot, by *the story that we are*. We've worked too much as a function of other people, or for other people, or for the idea we have of other people.

Kazbek says this doesn't change the fact that no editor will ever want to publish it.

And who says it's going to an editor? asks Mr. Peer. This work has a different path ahead of it.

✣

You and Mr. Peer pulled a good one, says Dacal as they walk across the sand to the sailboat. I suppose there's no harm in having a little fun like a pair of twenty year olds. But the world wants stories, as raw as they can be, full of facts and failures or fantastical reinterpretations of forgotten history. Epics, in short. Since you seem to have a thing for volcanoes these days, you could even write a novel about all of the volcanoes in Ecuador exploding at once. Villages destroyed. Mass exodus. A terrible catastrophe. Or do you think the novels being written these days are about more than using catastrophe to entertain couch potatoes? Don't fool yourselves. I'm happy you've had fun with your little game, but remember that things are moving in another direction.

Like the white cruise ship, says Kazbek.

Dacal asks what he means. Kazbek points to the cruise ship on the horizon and tells him.

✧

The artist's journey, Mr. Peer tells Kazbek, involves finding a teacher. During this journey, which lasts years, the artist formulates a precise list of questions inspired by works encountered along the way. Questions of a compositional, thematic, and moral nature. But artists never find a teacher. That's why their journey continues. And because they have already wandered too far and would lose too much time returning to their point of origin—or because they simply can't go back—they sit down to create in exile. When they begin to think what their work might be about, there is only one obvious answer: they will transcribe all the questions that they would have asked the teacher they never found. Once their work is done, they observe it and feel the urge to ask it questions, very different questions from the ones they had before. And the work, though they never suspect it, offers answers.

❁

Dacal smiles at the theory of the white cruise ship. You see too many ghosts, he says. He adds that he's still curious about what Kazbek will write from now on. I don't know, says Kazbek. He studies the shoreline and thinks about how he'll keep walking and connect his footsteps later. He says it aloud: *I'll keep walking and connect my footsteps later.* Like Mr. Peer's vermin? Dacal asks. Like Mr. Peer's vermin, says Kazbek.

❁

When it comes time to sail out, Dacal hugs him tight as if they were saying goodbye for a long time. But Kazbek suspects Dacal will show up again. He doesn't know when or where, but he knows how: in his own way.

Kazbek stays behind onshore, observing Dacal as he mounts the little wave runner that takes him off to the sailboat; then the boat sails away, impelled by gusts of wind, adapting to it even as it seems to brace against it. Kazbek bids him goodbye in silence, wishing him well, hoping that the sea will be good to him. The sailboat balances on the waves and leaves behind a trail of white foam that quickly disappears. What a difference from that rigid cruise ship, thinks Kazbek. Then, and only then, does a new and unexpected thought appear in Kazbek's mind: by observing Dacal's sailboat adapt to the wind, he has come to understand how the forces of chance work together.

❖

It's nighttime. He's cold. But this time the cold is real. Behind him is the highway that stretches from the center of Geneva to Lausanne. He makes a left and then a right, and then he's there, at Route de Valavran 85, standing before the low wall encircling the house that belongs to Isa's sister. He presses the buzzer, and the automatic gates open. He enters the garden and, there in the darkness, sees her in the door, ringed by the light spilling out from inside.

Isa pauses, then smiles. Get in here, she says. You're going to freeze out there in that cold.

ABOUT THE AUTHOR

Leonardo Valencia was born in Guayaquil, Ecuador, in 1969. He is the author of a short story collection, *La luna nómada* (1995), the novels *El desterrado* (2000), *El libro flotante* (2006), *Kazbek* (2008), and *La escalera de Bramante* (2019), and the essay collections *El síndrome de Falcón* (2008), *Viaje al círculo de fuego* (2014), and *Moneda al aire: sobre la novela y la crítica* (2017). His work has been included in over fifteen international anthologies and translated into English, French, Italian, Hebrew, and Bulgarian. In 2007 the Hay Festival de Bogotá 39 recognized him as one of Latin America's most prominent writers. He is a Professor of Literature and Creative Writing at the Universidad Andina Simón Bolívar in Quito.

ABOUT THE TRANSLATOR

Hillary Gulley is an award-winning translator of fiction and poetry from Spanish, Italian, and Portuguese. She has served as a guest editor for *Words Without Borders* and taught literary translation at Baruch College and Drew University. Her extensive work on Cuban writers has been anthologized, most recently, in *Island In The Light/Isla en la luz* (Tra Publishing, 2019).